Friendship

THE FOUR MUSICIANS

Adapted by Mary Rowitz

Illustrated by Wendy Edelson

Copyright © 2000 Publications International, Ltd.
ISBN: 0-7853-4311-3
Leap Frog is a trademark of Publications International, Ltd.

One day a donkey was walking along the fence by the barn, singing to himself. He stopped when he heard his owner talking with another farmer. The donkey leaned in closer so he could hear what the two were discussing.

"I know what you mean," the one farmer said. "Sometimes it's easier to just get a younger one."

The donkey wondered what they could be talking about. His owner continued, "I just can't find many reasons to keep the tired bag of bones around much longer. He's very old and cannot pull the plow anymore. It's time to put that old donkey out to pasture."

The donkey could not believe his ears! The farmers were talking about him! He was very hurt to hear these words. "Hee-haw!" said the donkey. "I won't be sent out to pasture. I'll go to the town of Bremen and become a great musician."

The donkey had just started on his way when he saw a sad dog sitting by the road. The donkey asked what was bothering the dog. "My owner says I am too old to hunt," howled the dog. "He wants to get a younger dog who keeps quiet."

"I have a thought that may interest you. Why don't you come with me to the town of Bremen, and we will work as musicians," said the donkey. "I'm sure we will be quite a team."

"Woof!" said the dog. "I really like that idea!" The two new pals had not gone far before they crossed paths with a gloomy cat. They asked what was wrong.

"My owner says I am too old to catch mice," he cried. "She is going to get a younger cat."

They invited the cat to come to Bremen to sing with them. "Mee-ow!" answered the cat, and the three were on their way.

The dog, cat, and donkey were walking along when suddenly a very upset rooster flew right into the middle of the road. "Cock-a-doodle-day!" the rooster squawked.

"What a strong voice you have!" the dog said.

"My owners say there is no point in having a strong voice if you don't use it every day," crowed the rooster. "I cannot seem to get up early enough to wake up the workers anymore. My owners plan to serve me for Sunday dinner!"

"Join us on our trip," said the dog. "We are going to work as musicians. We could really use your strong voice to make our band complete."

"Cock-a-doodle-day!" said the rooster. "Let's be on our way!" The four new friends practiced singing as they walked toward Bremen.

Nighttime came. The donkey, dog, cat, and rooster had been singing and walking all day. Soon the four musicians found a nice tree to camp under.

Just when they were falling asleep, the rooster began to squawk. "I think I see a light shining from inside a house!" he said. "It doesn't seem far away."

"They might have some good food to share with us," said the dog. "A big, juicy bone sounds mighty good right about now."

"Mmmm. I think a big bowl of milk would be absolutely purr-fect," purred the cat.

"A plate of corn certainly would hit the spot," crowed the rooster. The donkey thought it all sounded good, so the four set out for the house.

The four musicians walked up to the house. The donkey, being the tallest of the group, peered inside the window. "What do you see?" asked the cat.

"Well, there are four men sitting at a table that is covered with food," the donkey said. "They must eat like kings every night. There are stacks of gold everywhere."

"What do we do now?" asked the rooster. "Do we just knock on the door and ask for food?"

The donkey shook his head. "Remember we are going to be musicians," he said. "We should practice singing for our supper." The others thought this was a grand idea, so they carefully planned their first concert.

The four musicians decided to stand one on top of the other so everyone could be heard. First the donkey took his place near the bottom of the window. Then the dog jumped on his back. The cat made his way up to the dog's back. Finally the rooster flew to the top.

Even though the four friends had practiced their singing all day, they were still a little bit nervous. This was their first concert, after all. They wished each other good luck, turned to face the window, and cleared their throats. Finally their big moment had arrived. It was time to perform. The donkey gave the signal, and they began to sing.

Never has there been a louder or mightier group effort! The four friends tried to sing better than they ever had before. What they did not know is that it did not sound like singing. It sounded like, "Hee-haw! Woof! Mee-ow! Cock-a-doodle-day!"

The four friends also did not know that the men inside were robbers. When they heard the loud noise, they looked out the window and saw what looked like a four-headed beast. "Run! Run! Run!" one robber yelled. "Run before the four-headed beast gets us!"

The animals were confused. Why had the men run away? The donkey said, "I believe I know what they are doing. No doubt our audience enjoyed our singing so much that they must be going to get more people to hear our concert."

"It may be some time before they return. Let's go inside and have some dinner as a reward for our splendid singing," the rooster said.

"Indeed!" agreed the donkey. "That is a grand idea!" The four musicians went into the house.

The four musicians were so hungry that they ate every last bite! It didn't take long to decide that the life of a musician was going to suit them very well indeed. Soon after the meal, they were very sleepy. Since they were already inside the house, they agreed it would be best to spend the night there. After all, they didn't want to miss the people who were going to come hear them perform soon.

There was plenty of room for everyone in the house. The donkey lay in the middle of the room. The dog stretched out by the door. The cat curled up near the fireplace, and the rooster flew to a ceiling beam.

The four musicians lived in the house for the rest of their days. They were quite happy giving free concerts and using the gold to buy food.

The four musicians learned a great deal about friendship. At first they each felt sad and alone. Once they became friends with each other, they were much happier. When the four musicians started thinking about all the good things they could do together, they stopped feeling so sad.

How do you feel when a friend helps you? How do you feel when you help a friend? Is there someone you know who could use a friend?